KRISHNA AND SHISHUPALA

THE HOUSE OF KING DAMA-GHOSHA OF CHEDI* WAS STEEPED IN GLOOM. WHAT SHOULD HAVE BEEN A JOYOUS EVENT TURNED OUT TO BE A NIGHTMARE. THE LONG-AWAITED SON, BORN TO DAMAGHOSHA AND HIS QUEEN, WAS A FREAK, WITH FOUR ARMS AND THREE EYES.

AND HE SCREAMED AND BRAYED LIKE AN ASS.

STOP HIM! WHAT HAVE WE DONE TO DESERVE THIS?

EE..AW.. EE.. AW.. EE..AW

THE EVIL OMENS FRIGHTEN ME.

AH! HERE ARE THE PRIESTS AND THE ELDERS! THEY'LL TELL US WHAT TO DO.

* A VASSAL STATE OF MAGADHA

THE PRIESTS AND THE ELDERS HAD ALREADY DISCUSSED THE MATTER AMONG THEMSELVES.

ABANDON THE CHILD! THE EVIL OMENS DO NOT BODE WELL FOR THE KINGDOM...

THERE WAS A FLASH OF LIGHT AND A VOICE SUDDENLY CUT HIM SHORT.

O KING, THIS CHILD BRINGS YOU NO HARM. LOOK AFTER HIM. EVEN IF YOU ABANDON HIM, HE WILL NOT DIE...

...FOR HE IS DESTINED TO DIE ONLY AT THE HANDS OF THE ONE BORN TO SLAY HIM.

THE ANXIOUS MOTHER'S SHRIEK TORE THE SILENCE THAT FOLLOWED.

HOW WILL I KNOW THE SLAYER OF MY SON?

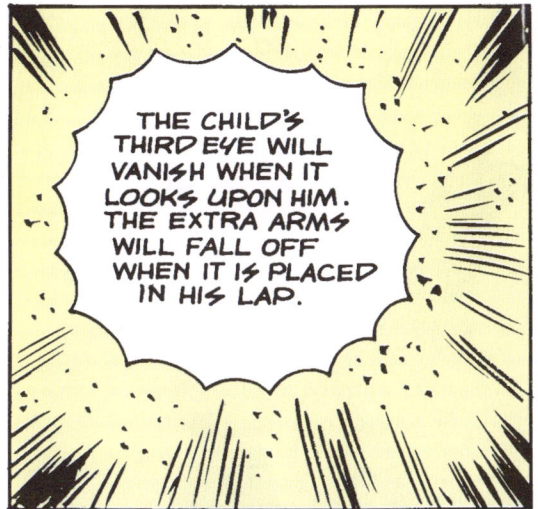

THE CHILD'S THIRD EYE WILL VANISH WHEN IT LOOKS UPON HIM. THE EXTRA ARMS WILL FALL OFF WHEN IT IS PLACED IN HIS LAP.

AND THE FLASH OF LIGHT WAS GONE!

MONTHS LATER, AT DWARAKA, BALARAMA CAME TO HIS BROTHER, KRISHNA, WITH NEWS.

SINCE WE KILLED KAMSA, THE EVIL SON-IN-LAW OF JARASANDHA,* NO EVENT HAS THROWN UP AS MUCH EXCITEMENT AS THIS!

AS WHAT?

AS THE BIRTH OF A MONSTER, TO OUR FATHER'S SISTER.

I SUPPOSE THEY'VE ABANDONED THE CHILD AS A FREAK?

NO! A VOICE DISSUADED THEM.

AND BALARAMA TOLD KRISHNA ALL THAT HE HAD HEARD.

* EMPEROR OF MAGADHA

THE CHILD HAS BEEN PLACED IN MANY A LAP. BUT SO FAR NOTHING HAS HAPPENED.

WE SHALL VISIT OUR AUNT.

I KNEW WE WOULD!

AND THE TWO BROTHERS SET OFF FOR THE CHEDI CAPITAL.

WHEN THEY REACHED THE PALACE AT CHEDI—

WELCOME, MY CHILD-REN. I HAVE BEEN EXPECTING YOU TO COME TO SEE YOUR LITTLE COUSIN.

SHE WENT OUT AND RETURNED WITH THE CHILD IN HER ARMS.

HOW CAN SHE HOLD IT SO LOVINGLY? I FIND IT REPULSIVE.

ISN'T HE A LOVELY, STRONG BABY?

4

THE NEXT MOMENT —

IT'S GONE! THE THIRD EYE IS GONE!

DELIGHTED TO SEE HER SON'S FACE NORMAL, THE TREMBLING QUEEN PLACED HIM IN KRISHNA'S LAP.

THE ARMS HAVE FALLEN OFF! HOW CUTE A BABY IS HE!

IN HER EXCESSIVE JOY THE SIGNIFICANCE OF THE EVENT ESCAPED HER. BUT ONLY FOR A MOMENT.

KRISHNA, TO THINK THAT IT SHOULD BE YOU? HIS OWN COUSIN!

O KRISHNA, I AM AFRAID! TERRIBLY AFRAID.

WILL YOU GRANT ME A BOON? YOU MUST NOT REFUSE!

I'LL TRY TO BRING YOU WHAT COMFORT I CAN.

PROMISE ME THAT YOU WILL PARDON, FOR MY SAKE, ANY OFFENCE GIVEN BY THIS CHILD.

FOR YOUR SAKE, I WILL PARDON HIS OFFENCES A HUNDRED TIMES, SO DON'T GRIEVE.

HE WILL PARDON HIM A HUNDRED TIMES! MY SON IS SAFE!

BUT DAMAGHOSHA WAS NOT SO CERTAIN. LONG AFTER KRISHNA AND BALARAMA LEFT HE WAS DEEP IN THOUGHT.

THE MIGHT OF KRISHNA IS MATCHED BY NONE BUT JARASANDHA, WHO IS NOW KRISHNA'S SWORN ENEMY. MY SON SHALL GROW UP AT THE COURT OF MAGADHA.

SO SHISHUPALA, AS THE CHILD WAS NAMED, WAS SENT TO MAGADHA.

A FINE BOY INDEED! I SHALL MAKE YOU A LION AMONG MEN.

IN THOSE DAYS RUKMI, THE PRINCE OF VIDARBHA*, WAS AN ADMIRER OF JARASANDHA AND WAS OFTEN AT HIS COURT.

RUKMI, THIS BOY HERE IS SHISHUPALA, MY WARD. TRAIN HIM TO BE AS GOOD A WARRIOR AS YOU ARE!

AS THE YEARS WENT BY, RUKMI AND SHISHUPALA BECAME CLOSE FRIENDS.

IF MY FATHER GIVES RUKMINI IN MARRIAGE TO SHISHUPALA, IT WOULD PLEASE THE EMPEROR AND BRING SHISHUPALA CLOSER TO ME.

* ANOTHER VASSAL STATE OF MAGADHA

BUT THE MUCH-SOUGHT-AFTER RUKMINI HAD OTHER PLANS. ONE DAY AT DWARAKA, BALA-RAMA SAW A BRAHMAN LEAVE, AND KRISHNA LOOKING THOUGHTFUL.

WHO WAS THAT BRAHMAN?

HE CAME WITH A MES-SAGE FROM THE PRINCESS OF VIDARBHA.

RUKMI'S SISTER, RUKMINI! THE GIRL WHO HAS WON YOUR HEART?

YES. HER BROTHER WANTS HER TO MARRY SHISHUPALA. BUT SHE HAS CHOSEN ME AND HER PARENTS SECRET-LY APPROVE. SHE WANTS ME TO CARRY HER AWAY.

AND KRISHNA SET OUT FOR VIDARBHA.

MEANWHILE, SHI-SHUPALA HAD ALREADY RECEIVED RUKMI'S FORMAL PROPOSAL.

THIS INDEED IS AN HONOUR! TO BE OFFERED THE HAND OF PEERLESS RUKMINI! AND NO SWAYAMWARA* TO FEAR!

* A CEREMONY WHERE A MAIDEN MAKES HER CHOICE, AMONG ASSEMBLED SUITORS, BY GARLANDING HIM.

BUT JARASANDHA WAS MORE CAUTIOUS.

I'LL HAVE TO BE ALERT! IT'S NO SECRET THAT KRISHNA WOULD HAVE MARRIED THE GIRL BUT FOR RUKMI. HE IS SURE TO TRY SOME WILY TRICK NOW.

IF HE DOES, IT'S GOING TO BE HARD FOR SHISHUPALA. I SHOULD KNOW! TO AVENGE KAMSA'S DEATH, EIGHTEEN TIMES HAVE I ENCOUNTERED HIM AND EIGHTEEN TIMES HAVE I FAILED!

A FEW DAYS LATER, BALARAMA RECEIVED ALARMING NEWS AT DWARAKA. HE SENT FOR HIS MEN.

THE EMPEROR HAS COMMANDED HIS ALLIES TO ASSEMBLE AT VIDARBHA. RALLY OUR ARMIES! WE'RE GOING TO VIDARBHA, TOO!

THE DAY OF THE WEDDING DAWNED. THE ASSEMBLY OF KINGS WAITED OUTSIDE THE TEMPLE WHERE RUKMINI HAD GONE TO PRAY BEFORE THE CEREMONY.

AH! THERE SHE COMES!

SHISHUPALA IS THE LUCKIEST MAN ON EARTH!

SUDDENLY —

KRISHNA! YOU'VE COME!

SHISHUPALA WAS THE FIRST TO REACT.

IT'S THAT COWHERD, KRISHNA! HE'S CARRYING AWAY MY BRIDE! STOP HIM! STOP HIM!

BUT SO BEMUSED WERE THE KINGS THAT THEY REMAINED ROOTED TO THE SPOT, GIVING KRISHNA A GOOD LEAD.

COME ON, O KINGS! SHALVA! POUNDRAKA! DANTA-VAKTRA! PURSUE THEM! WHERE IS YOUR KSHA-TRIYA SPIRIT?

WHY DON'T YOU MOVE? ALAS! SHAME ON US WHO FLAUNT OUR BOWS! A COWHERD HAS WHISKED HER AWAY LIKE A JACKAL SNATCHING THE PREY OF A LION.

WHEN WE ARE THERE, SHISHUPALA SHALL NOT LOSE HIS BRIDE. WE'LL RESCUE THE GIRL!

RUKMI'S WORDS WENT HOME. THE KINGS CHARGED FORWARD AND SOON CAUGHT UP WITH KRISHNA. AS THEY RAISED THEIR BOWS —

WAIT! I SHALL SHOOT THE FATAL ARROW! I HAVE TO VINDICATE MY HONOUR!

BUT SHISHUPALA'S ARROW MISSED ITS MARK. HE RAISED HIS BOW AGAIN.

THIS TIME I WILL NOT MISS!

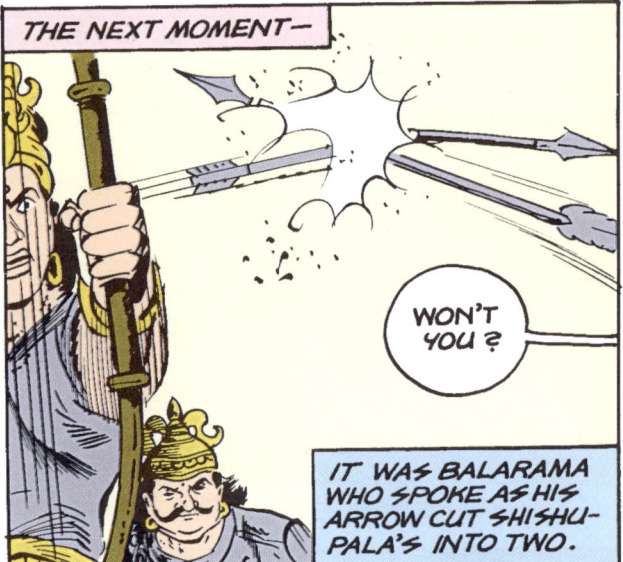

THE NEXT MOMENT—

WON'T YOU?

IT WAS BALARAMA WHO SPOKE AS HIS ARROW CUT SHISHU-PALA'S INTO TWO.

AS KRISHNA SPED AWAY WITH RUKMI IN HOT PURSUIT, BALARAMA AND HIS ARMY HELD THE OTHERS AT BAY.

A FIERCE BATTLE ENSUED. THE EMPEROR AND HIS ALLIES WERE ROUTED.

LUCK IS WITH THEM. IT'S NOT WISE TO FIGHT ANY LONGER. WE WILL HAVE TO RETREAT.

RUKMI HAS GONE AFTER THE COWHERD. HE MAY YET BRING BACK MY BRIDE. LET US FIGHT TILL HE RETURNS.

SHISHUPALA WAS RELUCTANT TO LEAVE THE BATTLEFIELD.

I KNOW KRISHNA AND I KNOW RUKMI TOO. THE GIRL IS GONE FOREVER.

AS THEY RODE AWAY FROM THE BATTLE-FIELD, SHALVA, THE KING OF SOUBHA, WHO COULD NOT BEAR SHISHUPALA'S PLIGHT, TOOK A VAIN OATH.

SHISHUPALA, ONE DAY I SHALL WIPE OUT THE RACE OF THE YADAVAS FROM THE FACE OF THIS EARTH. YOUR HUMILIATION SHALL NOT GO UN-AVENGED.

DANTAVAKTRA, ANOTHER VASSAL, SUPPORTED HIM.

AND HE'LL DO IT! COME, SHISHUPALA. DON'T GRIEVE.

TRYING TO CONSOLE THE DISTRAUGHT SUITOR AND BURNING WITH HATRED FOR HIS RIVAL ALL THE WHILE, THE VANQUISHED RETURNED TO THEIR CAPITALS.

AS HIS FATHER WAS NOW BEGINNING TO AGE, SHISHUPALA RETURNED TO CHEDI. WHEN HE ENTERED THE CAPITAL —

I HAD HOPED TO RETURN WITH A CHERISHED BRIDE BUT ALL I HAVE BROUGHT HOME IS HUMILIATION.

UNDER JARASANDHA'S PROTECTION, IN THE YEARS THAT FOLLOWED, SHISHUPALA OFTEN DELIBERATELY COMMITTED OFFENCES AGAINST THE YADAVAS — BUT ESCAPED UNPUNISHED.

HERE IS THAT RAT, SHISHUPALA! LET'S KILL HIM.

LET HIM GO, BALARAMA. REMEMBER MY PROMISE TO HIS MOTHER.

THEN ONE DAY, ONE OF SHISHU-PALA'S SPIES CAME WITH NEWS.

EMPEROR JARASANDHA HAS BEEN SLAIN!

OH, NO! WHO WAS THE WICKED MURDERER? THAT MIGHTY WARRIOR COULD NOT HAVE BEEN SLAIN IN A FAIR FIGHT.

THOUGH IT WAS PLANNED BY KRISHNA AND THE PANDAVAS, THE ACTUAL KILLING WAS BHIMA'S WORK.

THE FOUL DEED WAS DONE BY A PANDAVA! MY MOTHER'S SISTER'S CHILD! BUT WHAT DID HE HAVE AGAINST THE EMPEROR?

KING YUDHISHTHIRA WANTED TO PERFORM THE RAJASUYA SACRIFICE, FOR WHICH HE WOULD FIRST HAVE TO SECURE THE TITLE OF EMPEROR. JARASANDHA WAS THE ONLY OBSTACLE IN HIS PATH.

YUDHISHTHIRA'S FOUR BROTHERS, BHIMA ARJUNA, NAKULA AND SAHADEVA, ARE NOW ON THEIR WAY TO THE FOUR CORNERS OF THE EARTH TO SUBDUE THE KINGS. BHIMA WILL SOON BE COMING TO CHEDI.

AND IT WAS BHIMA WHO KILLED THE EMPEROR! WHAT SHOULD I DO?

AFTER PONDERING OVER THE MATTER, SHISHUPALA MADE A DECISION.

AFTER ALL, MY COUSIN YUDHISHTHIRA IS RENOWNED AS A VIRTUOUS KING. HE WILL ALWAYS BE FAIR IN HIS DEALINGS. I SHALL BECOME HIS VASSAL.

SO, WHEN BHIMA ARRIVED AT CHEDI, SHISHUPALA WENT OUT TO RECEIVE HIM.

WELCOME TO CHEDI, O MIGHTY WARRIOR! MY KINGDOM IS YOURS.

SURPRISED AND DELIGHTED BY THE WARM RECEPTION WHERE HE HAD EXPECTED HOSTILITY, BHIMA STAYED ON AT CHEDI FOR A MONTH, ENJOYING SHISHUPALA'S HOSPITALITY.

WHEN THE BROTHERS RETURNED HAVING BROUGHT ALL THE MAJOR KINGS UNDER HIS SWAY, SOME WILLINGLY, SOME BY FORCE, YUDHISHTHIRA SET A DATE FOR THE GRAND SACRIFICE IN CONSULTATION WITH KRISHNA AND THE ROYAL PRIESTS.

INVITATIONS WILL HAVE TO BE SENT OUT TO THE RISHIS, OUR COUSINS AT HASTINAPURA, THE ELDERS, AND THE VANQUISHED KINGS...

AT LAST THE GREAT DAY ARRIVED. THE SACRED RITUALS BEGAN. AS SHISHUPALA TOOK THE SEAT ASSIGNED TO HIM —

SHALVA AND DANTAVAKTRA ARE NOT HERE! DOES THE DEATH OF JARASANDHA STILL RANKLE IN THEM?

THE OFFICIATING PRIESTS GUIDED YUDHISHTHIRA THROUGH THE CEREMONIES TO THE FINAL DAY WHEN THE SOMA JUICE WAS EXTRACTED.

YOU MUST NOW DECIDE WHOM YOU WILL HONOUR FIRST IN THIS ASSEMBLY OF SAGES AND KINGS.

YUDHISHTHIRA WAS AT A LOSS. HE HAD THOUGHT OF EVERYTHING BUT THIS.

THERE ARE MANY PRESENT WHO ARE WORTHY OF THE PRIME HONOUR. WHAT SHALL I DO? WHOM SHALL I CHOOSE?

WHY DOES HE HESITATE? IS THERE ANY DOUBT TO WHOM THE HONOUR SHOULD GO?

WHEN YUDHISHTHIRA DID NOT SPEAK, SAHADEVA, THE YOUNGEST PANDAVA, STOOD UP.

I PROPOSE KRISHNA, THE PEERLESS! BY HONOURING HIM WE WILL HONOUR OURSELVES AND ALL CREATION.

AS YUDHISHTHIRA WAITED TENSELY FOR THE REACTION OF THE ASSEMBLY—

HEAR! HEAR!

WELL CHOSEN.

DEAR, DEAR KRISHNA! THOUGH NO ONE DESERVES THIS HONOUR MORE THAN YOU DO, IT IS GOOD TO SEE THAT EVERY-BODY APPROVES.

YUDHISHTHIRA ROSE . . .

. . . WASHED THE FEET OF KRISHNA . . .

. . . AND, AS WAS THE CUSTOM, SPRINKLED THE WATER IN WHICH HIS FEET HAD BEEN WASHED ON THE HEADS OF DRAUPADI AND HIS BROTHERS.

AS THE ASSEMBLY CHEERED LOUDLY, SHISHUPALA GREW LIVID WITH RAGE.

JAI! JAI!

SUDDENLY HIS VOICE CUT SHARPLY THROUGH THE CHEERS.

WAIT! HOW CAN YOU, THE ELDERS, THE WISE MEN OF THIS ASSEMBLY, SUCCUMB TO THE WHIMS OF A MERE BOY?

IT WAS SHISHUPALA. HE COULD NOT BEAR TO SEE HIS WORST ENEMY RECEIVING THE HIGHEST HONOUR.

HOW CAN YOU IGNORE THE CLAIMS OF YOUR WORTHIER GUESTS AND HONOUR THAT COWHERD?

FEEDING HIS FURY WITH EACH ABUSE, SHISHUPALA WENT ON.

ABANDONING THEIR OWN KINGDOM, THE YADAVAS HAVE TAKEN REFUGE IN AN ISLAND WHICH HAS NO BRAHMANS — NO VEDIC STUDIES. FROM THAT HIDEOUT THEY TYRANNISE VIRTUOUS KINGS.

HOW CAN ONE OF THIS BARBAROUS RACE BE WORTHY OF HONOUR, PARTICULARLY IN THIS AUGUST ASSEMBLY?

WHY DOESN'T KRISHNA STOP THIS MADMAN?

WHEN THE PANDAVAS AND THEIR ALLIES CHARGED AT SHISHUPALA TO SILENCE HIM —

SHAME ON YOU, NOBLE KSHATRIYAS, WHO WOULD DRAW YOUR SWORDS FOR A WILY COWHERD!

WAIT! SHISHUPALA IS DESTINED TO DIE AT MY HANDS. HONOURING A PROMISE MADE TO MY AUNT, HIS MOTHER . . .

. . . I HAVE PARDONED HIM A HUNDRED TIMES. HE HAS NOW EXCEEDED THAT NUMBER. HIS TIME IS UP.

SEEING THEIR SUZERAIN FALL, THE VASSAL CHIEFTAINS OF CHEDI FLED FOR THEIR LIVES.

QUICK! LET US ESCAPE AND CARRY THE NEWS TO SHALVA.

I'LL STAY BEHIND AND BRING NEWS OF THEIR PLANS.

WHEN THE CHIEFTAINS WHO HAD FLED, REACHED SHALVA'S COURT —

SHISHUPALA HAS BEEN SLAIN!

IT WAS THAT VILE YADAVA COWHERD, KRISHNA, WHO DID IT.

SORROW AND ANGER OVERCAME SHALVA.

HE STOLE MY FRIEND'S BRIDE AND NOW HE HAS TAKEN HIS VERY LIFE. WHERE IS KRISHNA?

JUST THEN THE CHIEFTAIN WHO HAD STAYED BACK, ENTERED —

HE IS STILL AT INDRAPRASTHA. YUDHISHTHIRA ASKED HIM TO STAY ON AFTER THE SACRIFICE.

21

AND BALARAMA?

HE, TOO, IS AT INDRA-PRASTHA.

NOW IS THE TIME TO RAZE DWARAKA AND FULFIL MY PLEDGE. I WILL EXTERMINATE THE YADAVAS. AND LORD SHIVA WILL HELP ME DO IT.

SHALVA PERFORMED SEVERAL PENANCES TO APPEASE LORD SHIVA. WHEN SHIVA AT LAST APPEARED BEFORE HIM—

O LORD, GIVE ME A CHARIOT THAT CAN BECOME INVISIBLE AT MY COMMAND AND THAT CAN TRAVEL ON WATER, AIR AND EARTH ALIKE.

YOU SHALL HAVE IT. MAYA* WILL BRING IT TO YOU.

AS SOON AS SHALVA RECEIVED THE CHARIOT, HE ADDRESSED HIS MEN.

GET READY TO MOUNT AN ATTACK ON DWARAKA, THE CITY OF THE YADAVAS. WE WILL LEAVE FORTHWITH.

* ARCHITECT OF THE DEVAS AND ASURAS

WHEN SHALVA AND HIS ARMY REACHED DWARAKA —

YOU LAY SIEGE TO THE CITY WHILE I ATTACK FROM THE SKIES.

SHALVA DID NOT WASTE ANY TIME. SOARING INTO THE SKIES IN HIS CHARIOT, HE SHOWERED STONES, TREES, SNAKES, WATER AND EARTH OVER THE CITY, WREAKING HAVOC UPON IT.

THE CITIZENS OF DWARAKA RUSHED IN ALARM TO PRADYUMNA.*

LORD! LORD! WE ARE BEING ATTACKED... FROM THE SKIES!

* KRISHNA'S SON

WHERE? BY WHOM?

WE DON'T KNOW. WE CAN'T SEE ANYONE DISPATCHING WEAPONS.

THE SKIES ARE CLOAKED IN DARKNESS.

DON'T PANIC! I'LL PROTECT YOU.

AND PRADYUMNA RODE OUT.

MEANWHILE AT INDRAPRASTHA, KRISHNA AWOKE WITH A START.

BALARAMA! DWARAKA IS IN TROUBLE! WE MUST RETURN IMMEDIATELY.

UH? DWARAKA?

BIDDING YUDHISHTHIRA AND HIS BROTHERS FAREWELL, KRISHNA AND BALARAMA LEFT FOR DWARAKA.

AS THEY APPROACHED THEIR CITY —

LOOK! IT'S SHALVA! HE HAS ATTACKED THE CITY WHILE WE WERE AWAY.

GO, BALARAMA. HELP PRADYUMNA GUARD THE CITY. PROTECT FATHER. I'LL DEAL WITH SHALVA.

AS BALARAMA RODE INTO THE CITY, PRADYUMNA MET HIM.

AH! YOU'RE BACK. WE'VE ALMOST FINISHED OFF SHALVA'S ARMY. I'VE KILLED SHALVA'S MINISTER. NOW I'M GOING TO GET HIM.

NO. LEAVE HIM TO YOUR FATHER. WE'LL GUARD THE CITY AND PROTECT YOUR GRANDFATHER.

MEANWHILE, KRISHNA HAD FOUND SHALVA.

DRIVE THE CHARIOT NEAR HIS. HE IS A SKILLED MAGICIAN. SO DON'T BE FRIGHTENED BY ANYTHING YOU SEE.

IN FACT IT WAS SHALVA WHO WAS FRIGHTENED FOR A MOMENT.

IT'S KRISHNA! AND MY ARMY IS ALMOST ANNIHILATED! MY MINISTER IS DEAD. I'LL HAVE TO USE MY MOST POWERFUL WEAPON—THE SHAKTI.

AND SHALVA HURLED THE SHAKTI ...

... BUT KRISHNA SMASHED IT TO BITS WITH HIS SWIFT, WELL-AIMED ARROWS.

I'LL DESTROY FOREVER THE BOW THAT SENT THOSE ARROWS AND THE HAND THAT WIELDED IT!

WITH A TRIUMPHANT ROAR, SHALVA MADE FOR KRISHNA.

STEAL MY FRIEND'S BRIDE, WOULD YOU? SLAY HIM, WOULD YOU? TODAY I SHALL SEND YOU TO THE JAWS OF DEATH — YOU WHO BOAST OF NEVER HAVING BEEN DEFEATED!

BUT THE NEXT MOMENT, KRISHNA SWUNG OUT WITH HIS MACE AND HIT SHALVA.

EE-A-A-AH!

AS SHALVA FELL KRISHNA DIPPED HIS CHARIOT IN HOT PURSUIT.

BUT THE MOMENT SHALVA'S BODY TOUCHED THE EARTH, IT VANISHED.

AND A FEW MINUTES LATER, A MAN STOOD BEFORE KRISHNA, HIS HEAD BOWED, HIS EYES STREAMING WITH TEARS.

I HAVE BEEN SENT BY DEVAKI*. O KRISHNA, SHALVA HAS CARRIED AWAY YOUR FATHER!

IT CANNOT BE TRUE! HOW COULD SHALVA DEFEAT BALA-RAMA, AND CARRY AWAY MY FATHER! BALA-RAMA, WHOM EVEN THE DEVAS AND ASURAS CAN'T DEFEAT!

SUDDENLY—

LOOK, KRISHNA! I'VE GOT YOUR FATHER! I PLAN TO KILL HIM BEFORE YOUR VERY EYES! IF YOU ARE POWERFUL ENOUGH, SAVE HIM.

SO WHAT I HEARD WAS TRUE!

* KRISHNA'S MOTHER

AND SHALVA BROUGHT HIS SWORD DOWN ON HIS CAPTIVE'S NECK.

AS SHALVA MOUNTED HIS CHARIOT AND ROSE INTO THE AIR, KRISHNA WHO WAS FOR A MOMENT STUNNED, SUDDENLY REALISED THE TRUTH.

SHALVA HAS CAST A SPELL ON ME. IT'S AN ILLUSION. THERE WAS NO MESS-ENGER AND MY FATHER IS SAFE.

AND LO! EVEN AS KRISHNA SAW THE TRUTH, THE CORPSE AS WELL AS THE MESSEN-GER VANISHED.

AH! THERE HE IS! I WILL NOT SPARE HIM NOW!

HE HAS FOUND ME OUT!

QUICK! TAKE THE CHARIOT AS CLOSE TO HIM AS YOU CAN.

IF I HAVE TO DESTROY SHALVA, I'LL FIRST HAVE TO DESTROY HIS CHARIOT.

THE NEXT MOMENT, SWINGING OUT HIS MACE, WITH ONE BLOW KRISHNA SHATTERED SHALVA'S CHARIOT.

UNDAUNTED, SHALVA CAME OUT OF THE WATER...

...AND CHARGED AT KRISHNA WITH HIS MACE.

REPELLING THE ATTACK WITH ONE HAND . . .

. . . KRISHNA HELD UP THE OTHER FOR HIS DISCUS . . .

. . . AND SENT IT FLYING TOWARDS SHALVA.

SHALVA FELL, HIS HEAD SEVERED FROM THE BODY.

HAVING SLAIN ALL THE MAJOR ENEMIES OF THE YADAVAS, KRISHNA ENTERED HIS CITY CHEERED BY HIS JUBILANT SUBJECTS.

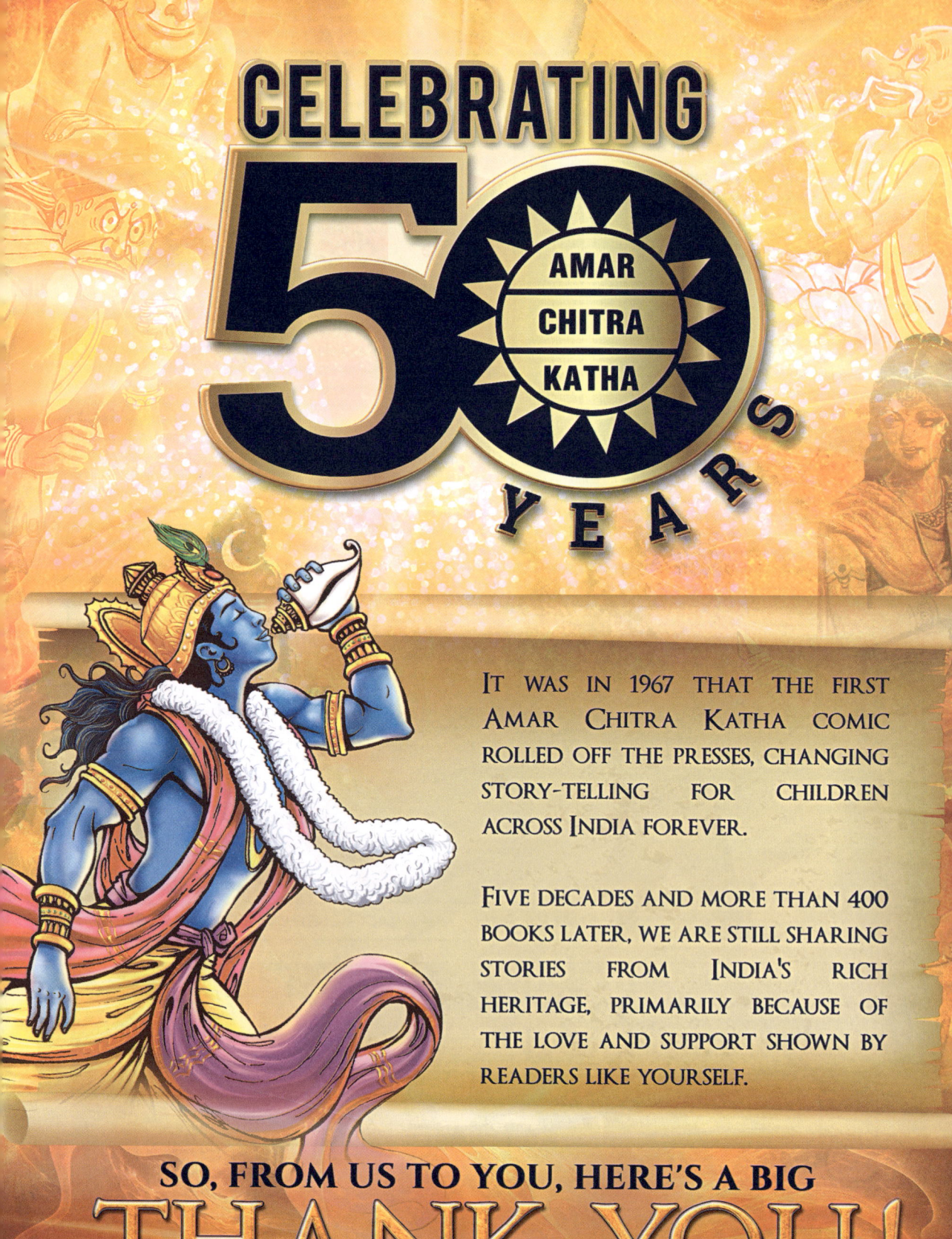